Designed by
Nicola Butler

First published in 2022 by Usborne Publishing Ltd., Usborne House, 83-85 Saffron Hill, London EC1N 8RT England.
usborne.com Copyright © 2021 Usborne Publishing Ltd. The name Usborne and the Balloon logo are Trade Marks
of Usborne Publishing Ltd. All rights reserved. No part of this publication may be reproduced, stored in a retrieval
system, or transmitted in any form or by any means without the prior permission of Usborne Publishing Ltd. UKE.

I'm (almost) NEVER BORED

Anna Milbourne

Illustrated by Åsa Gilland

I'm hardly ever bored –
I'm a busy, busy bee most of the time.

There's school and dance class
and ukulele lessons, and then there's
screen time – with SO MANY cartoons
to watch and games to play.

But when Daddy says, "That's enough
screen time for now, sweetheart..."

...the fun STOPS, and everything feels SLOW and BORING.
I have **nothing whatsoever** to do!

So I ask Daddy,
"Will you play a game with me?"
"Maybe later," Daddy says. "I have to
unpack these boxes. Can you play
by yourself for a little bit?"
I let out a wail,

"I'm **BOOOORED!**"

You know what Daddy says? "Oh, that's great!" – AND he's even SMILING! Then he says, "You see, being bored comes RIGHT BEFORE having a Really Good Idea."

I sigh loudly. But then a big box catches my eye. What if... What if it's NOT just a box. It could be a...

Mr. Unicorn and I pop out to see.
It's a land of wibbly-wobbly jellies!

So we BOUNCE...

BOUNCE...

BOUNCE around on them.

"READY?

W

Next we come to a wavy-wavy sea full of sharks!

We find a boat and we ROW, ROW, ROW.

Then we jump onto clouds.

And we FLOAT...

FLOAT...

FLOAT...

...along until we find a magic door. We slip through the door, back home to Daddy.

Next day, it's Mummy's turn to look after me, but she has to work. "Mummy, will you play with me?" I ask.

"Not just now, sweetie - I have to finish this!" she says.

"I'm SO **BORED!**" I moan.

And Mummy says, "It's okay to be bored sometimes. Being bored comes right before having a Really Good Idea..."

"I don't HAVE a good idea," I say crossly,
and draw a big, angry scribble.

I stare at my
scribble.

It looks a bit like
a tangly SPAGHETTI
monster!

What if...

...What if it was **real?!**

It looks like a VERY **HUNGRY** spaghetti monster.

Quickly, I draw one,

two,

three,

four grapes

and a very big orange,

some cupcakes,

a slice of pizza

and a GIANT ICE CREAM.

But the monster STILL looks hungry. It might eat me up too! I escape from my drawing back to...

...Mummy, who is saying, "Time for lunch!" And guess what we're having?

Another day, I'm helping Daddy to do the laundry. I can't think of anything to play.

"I'm **BORED!**" I groan.

And Daddy says, "That's okay. Being bored comes right before a Really Good..."

But I'm not listening any more. I'm watching the washing go round and round. WHAT IF...

...we were spinning through space!

"COME ON MR. UNICORN!" I cry, and we whizz past a planet of odd socks...

...I crash land RIGHT
BACK in my own garden
...BOING!

I'm lying there, wondering what to do next, and I'm just
ABOUT to feel bored when I notice some teensy bugs,
all marching through a gap in the grass.

And I wonder: WHAT IF...

I was teensy
and they were
HUGE!